*Other Kipper books:*

KIPPER
KIPPER'S TOYBOX
KIPPER'S BIRTHDAY
KIPPER'S BOOK OF COUNTING
KIPPER'S BOOK OF COLOURS
KIPPER'S BOOK OF OPPOSITES
KIPPER'S BOOK OF WEATHER
WHERE, OH WHERE, IS KIPPER'S BEAR?
KIPPER'S SNOWY DAY
KIPPER'S CHRISTMAS EVE
KIPPER'S A TO Z
KIPPER AND ROLY
KIPPER'S BALLOON
KIPPER'S BEACH BALL

THE LITTLE KIPPER SERIES
THE LITTLE KIPPER COLLECTION
KIPPER STORY COLLECTION
THE 2ND LITTLE KIPPER COLLECTION

First published 2002
This paperback edition first published 2003
by Hodder Children's Books,
a division of Hodder Headline Limited,
338 Euston Road, London NW1 3BH

Copyright © Mick Inkpen 2002

10 9 8 7 6 5

ISBN 0340 84177 X PB

Printed in Hong Kong

# Kipper's Monster

## Mick Inkpen

h
Hodder
Children's
Books

A division of Hodder Headline Limited

Tiger had a brand new torch.
    'It's the most powerful torch
there is!' he said to Kipper.
He shone it at Big Owl.
    He shone it at Hippo.
        He shone it in Kipper's face.
    'You should see it when it's
dark!' he said. 'It's REALLY good
when it's dark!'

He sat in Kipper's basket and pulled the blanket over his head.

'Come on! We can make it dark under here!' he said.

Under the blanket was one of Kipper's storybooks.

'That's another thing!' said Tiger. 'You can read under the bedclothes with a torch like this!'

Kipper began to read.
'Deep in the middle of the dark, dark wood, there lived a horrible, horrendous, terrible, tremendous . . .'

'That's it!' shouted Tiger, jumping up. 'We'll camp in the woods tonight! It'll be really, REALLY dark in the woods.'

'Shall I bring my book?' said Kipper.

So they took the book, and some biscuits, and they put up their tent in the middle of the woods, at the bottom of Big Hill.

But as it began to get dark Tiger began to think that perhaps it wasn't such a good idea after all.

'Come inside and have a biscuit,' said Kipper. 'Do you want Rabbit or Big Owl?'

But Tiger didn't reply. He was looking nervously out of the door. 'Do you think there are any bears in these woods?' he whispered.

'No, I shouldn't think so,' said Kipper. He began to read.

'Deep in the middle of the dark, dark wood, there lived a horrible. . .'

But Tiger wasn't ready. He asked Kipper to sit next to the door, instead of him. And when Kipper tried again to read, Tiger got up and zipped the door shut altogether.

But the third time Kipper tried to read, from somewhere outside the tent, there came the most terrible, tremendous, horrible, horrendous,

'Screech!'

'What was that?' said Kipper. Tiger said nothing.

'Let's go and look!' whispered Kipper. So they crept out of the tent and into the woods, shining Tiger's torch ahead of them.

'I think it came from somewhere near here,' said Kipper. The torch beam lit up the enormous, grey trunk of an old tree.

There in the middle was a dark, dark hole.

S uddenly a huge pair of
yellow eyes blinked open, and
from the hole came the most terrible,

'Screech!'

They shrieked and ran, bumping
into each other and sending the
torch flying. They scrambled into the
tent and lay there panting hard,
listening. . .

'I think it was just an owl,' whispered Kipper. 'Yes, it was just a silly, old owl.'

But behind him, the shadow of something was growing on the wall of the tent.

Something with horns.

'It's a horrible, horrendous monster!' squealed Tiger.

The shape on the tent, grew and grew till it was looming above them. Then it slowly changed into a shape that Kipper had seen before.

Kipper crept back out of the tent and walked towards the torchlight. There, caught in the beam, was a little snail.

Kipper picked up the torch and let the snail crawl onto his paw. He looked at the snail closely.

Its horns curled in and out as he touched them.

'I've found the horrible, horrendous monster! Look Tiger!'

Tiger peeped out from underneath the blanket.

He saw the snail.

He saw its shadow.

He felt silly.

'Shall I read the story now?' said Kipper.

But Kipper never did get to read
his story, because they went
home to Tiger's house, where they
put up the tent in Tiger's bedroom. . .

. . .and Tiger got to read it instead.